The Kitten
with
No Name

The Kitten
with
No Name

Vivian French

Illustrated by
Selina Young

Orion
Children's Books

The Kitten With No Name originally
appeared in *The Story House*
first published in Great Britain in 2004
by Orion Children's Books
This edition first published in 2009
by Orion Children's Books
a division of the Orion Publishing Group Ltd
Orion House
5 Upper St Martin's Lane
London WC2H 9EA
An Hachette UK Company

A catalogue record for this book
is available from the British Library

Printed and bound in China

ISBN 978 1 4440 0077 1

To dearest Nat,
love from Gumble

x x

One

Once there was a kitten without a name. He was born under a hedge, so he had no home either.

"Mee**OW**," said his mother.
"When you are big enough we will
go out into the world. I'll take you
somewhere very special where we
can live happily ever after."

"How will we know when we've
found the right place?" asked the kitten.

His mother began to purr.

"We'll know," she said.
"We'll feel warm and cosy
and someone will
love us."

"That sounds good," said the kitten and he snuggled into the dry leaves and went to sleep.

The kitten grew bigger. Every day he asked his mother if he was big enough to go out into the world and every day she said, "Not yet."

"We're going to find somewhere special where we can live happily ever after," said the kitten. "Aren't we, Mother?"

"That's right," said his mother. "Somewhere very special."

"Why is it special?" asked the kitten.

"Well," said his mother, "it'll be special because it'll be our very own home."

"Our own home!" the kitten said. "That sounds good. Will it keep out the wind and the rain?"

"It certainly will," his mother told him. "There'll be a roof and walls."

The kitten snuggled down against his mother's warm side. "Tell me again how we'll know the right place," he said.

"We'll feel warm and cosy," said his mother and she licked his ears.

"You've forgotten the best bit," said the kitten.

"Oh yes," said his mother. "And someone will love us. They'll love us very much."

"That's right," said the kitten and he began to purr.

"Purr ... purr ... purr."

Two

Every day the kitten with no name scrambled out from under the hedge where he lived to play with the waving buttercups and to catch the dancing daisies. Every day he chased the butterflies that went flittering past.

"Be careful," said his mother. "Don't go too far."

"I'll be careful," said the kitten.

One day the kitten found an old
conker. He patted it and it skittered
across the ground.

The kitten bounced after it –
straight into a group of children who
were on their way to the park nearby.

"Oh!" said a tall boy. "Look! What a
pretty kitten!" And he picked the kitten
up and hugged him.

"H'm," thought the kitten.
"Being hugged is good. I've never
been hugged before."

He began to purr loudly.
"Purr ... purr ... PURR."

"Want to see the kitty," said
a very little girl.

The tall boy held out the
kitten for her to see.

"Pretty kitty," said
the little girl. "Take
him home?"

"No, Daisy B," said the tall boy.
"We've already got

Fat Freda

and Big Tom

and there's Granny
Annie's Kitty Purr too –
there's no room
for another cat."

The very little girl began to cry.
"Want the kitty! Daisy B wants
the kitty! Daisy B wants a kitty of
her very own!"

"Come on," said the tall boy and he
put the kitten down. "Let's go to the
park – I'll push you on the swings."

"Yes!" shouted the very little girl.
She turned to wave to the kitten.
"Bye bye, pretty kitty. See you soon."
And all the children ran off.

The kitten ran back to his mother
under the hedge.

"Mother," he said. "I was hugged!"

"Hugging is good if it isn't too tight," said his mother.

"It wasn't too tight," the kitten said. "It was nice. And a little girl wanted to take me home!"

His mother jumped to her feet and her fur bristled.

"You must *never* let anyone take you home," she said.

"We're going to go to our own home!"

"I know," said the kitten. "And it will be warm and cosy and someone will love us."

"That's right," said his mother.

The kitten looked hopeful. "Will we be hugged?"

"Of course," said his mother. "Now wash your paws and whiskers and I'll tuck you up."

The kitten curled up in his little leafy bed. "I think," he said sleepily, "I shall dream about being hugged."

And he shut he eyes and began
to purr.

Three

One day the kitten who had no name was chasing a big white butterfly. He chased it up and he chased it down and then he stopped. His mother was calling him.

"Be a good kitten," she said, "and stay right here by our hedge today. I'm going to go up to the end of the field to see what I can see and I may be a little while."

"Are you going to find our special place?" asked the kitten hopefully. "The very special place you told me about? The very special place where we can live happily for ever and ever and be hugged?"

"Not today," said his mother. "But very very soon. I'm just going to see how the weather will be tomorrow." And off she went.

The kitten watched the big white butterfly flitter out of reach and then he sat down to think.

"I'm big enough to go to the end
of the field," he thought.

And then he thought, "I could give
Mother a surprise! If she sees that I'm
big enough to go to the end of the
field, she'll see that I'm big enough to
go with her and find our new home.

And maybe—" the kitten jumped
up "—we could go today!"

The kitten was so excited that
he began to skip up and down.

"*Yes!*" he said to himself. "*Yes!*
I'll run after Mother and then she'll see
what a big grown-up cat I am – and we'll
find the very special place in time to go
to bed!" And he scrambled away from
the hedge where he and his mother
had lived ever since he was born.

Off he went,
the way his
mother had
gone.

The grass in the field was long and thick. The kitten had not been there often; he usually stayed on the other side of the hedge where children played and the grass was short.

"Mee**OW,** I can't see where to go," he said.

He **jumped**
and he **bounded**
and **leapt**.

And he **leapt**
and he **bounded**
and he **jumped**.

And he **bounded**
and he **leapt**
and he **jumped**.

And he **bounded**.

 27

And he stopped.

"I'm tired," said the kitten and he was. His paws hurt and there was grass seed in his fur.

"I think I'll go back now," said the kitten.

He turned
himself round
and round and
then round
again.

"Which way do I go?"
he thought. "Is it this way?"
But it wasn't.

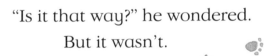

"Is it that way?" he wondered.
But it wasn't.

"It must be this way," said the kitten.
But it wasn't.

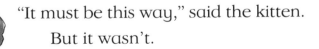

29

"Oh dear," said the kitten and he sat down under a large thistle. "I think I'm lost." Two big tears rolled down his nose.

There was a rustling in the grass and a squeaking.

The kitten sniffed loudly. "Mother?" he said hopefully.

A mouse popped her head from out under a thistle leaf.

"Oh my whistling whiskers!" she said. "It's a kitten!"

The kitten sniffed again.
"Hello," he said. "Have you
seen my mother?"

"No," said
the mouse. She
looked nervously
over her shoulder.

"Is she near?"

"I don't know,"
said the kitten.
"I'm lost."

"Oh." The mouse sat down beside
him. "Where do you live?"

"Under a big green hedge," said
the kitten. "But I don't know which
way to go."

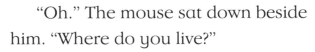

"A big hedge?" said the mouse. "That's easy. You see that yellow gorse bush over there?"

The kitten looked. "Yes," he said.

"The big hedge is just a step and a hop further on," said the mouse and she twitched her tail and skipped away.

"Thank you!" said the kitten
and he began jumping ...

and **bounding** ...

and **leaping** ...

all the way to the
yellow gorse bush.

When he got there he stopped. Yes! There in front of him was a big hedge.

"*Hurrah!*" said the kitten. "I'll soon be back now." He yawned. "But I'm very tired. Maybe I'll have a little sleep. Mother won't be there just yet."

He crept under the shelter of the gorse bush and curled himself up into a neat little ball.

"**Purr**," he said to himself.
"This is a very pretty bush. I wonder
why I didn't see it before?"

And he closed his eyes and began
to dream of a very special place
covered in pretty yellow flowers …
a warm and cosy place to live in for
ever and ever.

Four

The kitten who had no name slept
and slept. When he woke up it was
getting late.

"Mee**OW!**" said the kitten.
He stood up and stretched.

"I must hurry. Mother's sure to be back by now. Which way is my hedge?"

He looked about and there, sure enough, was a big green hedge. It wasn't far away at all.

"I'd better hurry," said the kitten. He ran with a hop and a skip and a jump and he didn't look where he was going.

Splash

The kitten fell into a stream.

The water was very very cold …
and the kitten couldn't swim.

"**Meeeeow!**" he shrieked.

"**Meeeeow!**

Mother! Mother!

Meeeeow!"

Down and down he sank and then
up and up he bobbed again.

Down and down …

"Flip my flippers," said
a croaky voice.

Someone or something seized
the kitten by the scruff of the neck.
Someone or something pulled him
out of the stream.

"Flip my flippers and what have we got here?"

The kitten opened his eyes.

A large green frog was standing in front of him.

"You should learn to swim, young animal," said the frog. "You could drown yourself jumping in like that."

He began to rub the kitten's wet fur with a handful of grass.

"Not that it wasn't a good jump. Not as good as us frogs do, of course, but not bad. Not bad at all." He picked another handful of grass.

The kitten gave a feeble mew. The frog was steadily rubbing him dry again, but he still felt cold.

The frog suddenly stopped.

"Dear me! Are you meant to be furry?" he asked.

The kitten nodded.

"That's all right, then." The frog went on rubbing. "I wondered if the water had done something funny to your scales. Or your feathers."

He gave the kitten a final pat.

"Go on, then.

Tell us what you are."

"I'm a kitten," said the kitten. "I was trying to get back to my mother, but the stream got in the way." And he began to cry.

"Now now now," said the frog. "We don't need tears. Tears never sorted anything. What we need is action!"

"Do we?" asked the kitten.

The frog nodded. "I'll get you sorted out – no trouble. You just curl up here by the dandelions. I'll go and get my friend. He'll take you over the stream – no trouble."

The kitten yawned. He did feel tired and the evening sun was beginning to feel warm and comfortable on his back.

"Thank you very much," he said and he curled himself up by the dandelions. "Will your friend really help me?"

"Sure as tadpoles turn into frogs," said the frog. He hopped away – and then he jumped back.

"Hey – no more swimming. Right?"

"Right," said the sleepy kitten.

"Good," said the frog and
he jumped into the stream
with a

plop

The kitten yawned again. "I'll soon be back with my mother," he thought. "We'll soon be together again … and then we can find our very special place … all warm and cosy … and someone there will love us and hug us …" and he drifted off to sleep.

Five

"*Quack!*" The kitten woke up with a start. A duck was standing beside him.

"*Quack!*" The duck peered at the kitten. "Are you a kitten?"

The kitten nodded.

"Good," said the duck. "Frog says you need to cross the stream."

"Oh yes, please!" said the kitten. "Are you Frog's friend? He pulled me out of the water when I fell in!"

There was a loud splash, and Frog came leaping up the bank.

"Kitten," he said, "this is Duck. Duck, my friend, can you take this young fellow over the stream? He lives in the big green hedge over there."

The duck looked surprised.

"I didn't know kittens lived in trees," she said.

The kitten shook his head. "I live under the hedge," he said, "not in it. Can you really take me? I do so want to see my mother."

"Could he sit on your back, Duck?" asked the frog.

"I think I'd sink," the duck said. "Couldn't he sit on a lily leaf? If he sat on a lily leaf we could push it across."

"Flip my flippers!" said the frog. "What a brain! Two ticks, and I'll be back."

He dived into the water, and swam to a patch of lilies. He chose the biggest leaf, and swam back towing it behind him.

"Here you are, young fellow. Hop on!"

The kitten went nervously down to the edge of the stream.

"Ooooooh!"

he said, as he felt the lily pad tremble underneath his paws. "I don't like it!"

"Try shutting your eyes," said the frog. "Now, Duck – are you ready? Away we go!"

The kitten shut his eyes tightly. He held his breath as the lily pad moved slowly across the stream. The duck pushed behind, and the frog towed in front.

"Nearly there!" said the frog. "Nearly there!" He gave the lily pad a huge heave.

The lily pad wobbled.

"Meow!" howled the kitten, and he held on as tightly as he could.

"Quack!" said the duck.

"Calm down, young kitten.
Here we are!"

The kitten felt the lily pad touch the
bank with a small bump.

"Oh – meeeeeOW!"
he said. He jumped onto dry land,
and turned round. "Thank you!
Thank you!" he said.
"I'll never forget you!"
"No trouble at all!"
said the frog, and he
and the duck waved as
the kitten went hurrying
away towards the
big green
hedge.

"Mother!" the kitten called. "Mother! I'm here!"

There was no answer.

The kitten scampered across the grass – and then stopped and stared.

It wasn't his hedge.

There were sandy holes in among the roots, just like where he lived, but he knew it was wrong. It was terribly wrong.

The kitten sat down and cried.

"Meow!" he wailed. **"Meow!"**

"Sh!" said a voice. "Sh! You'll wake my babies!"

The kitten spun round.

Behind him was a rabbit. "Oh, please be quiet!" she said. "They've only just gone to sleep!"

"I'm very sorry," said the kitten. "I didn't mean to wake them … but I'm lost!"

"Lost?" The rabbit looked horrified. "But you should be at home. It's getting late!"

"I know," said the kitten, "but this isn't my hedge. I thought it was, but it isn't. It looks just like it – but it's different."

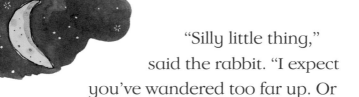

"Silly little thing," said the rabbit. "I expect you've wandered too far up. Or too far down. As long as you stay near the hedge you'll find your way. The hedge goes all the way round the field, you know. Just keep looking." And she popped back down into her hole with a whisk of her white fluffy tail.

"Oh!" The kitten suddenly felt much better. "Oh! I see! If I walk along beside the hedge I'll find Mother for certain!"

Pop!

The rabbit was back out.

"A little thing like you really shouldn't be out so late," she said.

"Quick! Creep down here, and you can stay for the night. You can find your way back in the morning. Can't have you wandering about in the dark – wouldn't sleep a wink for worrying! Come along down – and mind you tiptoe. I don't want those babies woken up!"

The kitten didn't argue. It was getting very dark, and there were strange, rustly noises that made him shiver. He tiptoed after the rabbit, and found himself in a warm burrow filled with soft grass.

"There!" she said. "No nonsense, now – clean your whiskers and go to sleep. You'll find your mother in the morning."

"Thank you," whispered the kitten. He snuggled down in the grass … and three little baby bunnies snored and snuffled beside him.

"I'll find Mother in the morning," the kitten told himself. "And she'll tell me about our very special place … our home which is warm and cosy … where we'll be hugged …" He began to purr.

"Sh," said the rabbit, but she said it very softly.

Six

The kitten woke up feeling bright and cheerful. The three baby bunnies were still fast asleep, but Mother Rabbit was bustling about, tidying up.

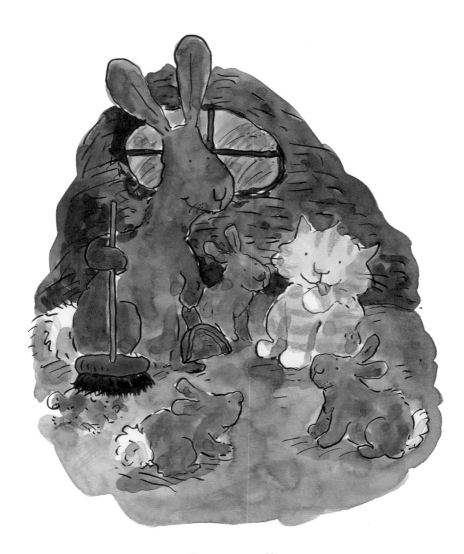

"There's a good little kitten," she said when she saw him beginning to wash his paws. "Now, when you've finished washing you can come and have some breakfast, and then you must run along and find your mother. She must be worried sick about you!"

The kitten nodded, and gave his paws one last lick.

"I'm ready!" he said. "And I'm hungry."

"That's good," said the rabbit, and she gave him a very small carrot.

The kitten's whiskers drooped.

"Oh," he said, as politely as he could. "Thank you."

He tried hard to eat the carrot, but he didn't like it much.

"There there," said the rabbit as she swept up the bits. "I expect you're missing your mother."

"Yes," said the kitten, and he nodded hard.

The rabbit patted his head. "Time to run along," she said.

"Keep going the same direction, and you're sure to find your way. Don't go talking to any strange animals, and keep near the hedge!"

"I will," said the kitten. He looked round the burrow. It suddenly felt very warm and cosy, and the world outside seemed very big.

"Now now," said the rabbit, "you'll be fine."

"Yes," said the kitten. "And thank you
very very much for looking after me."

The rabbit looked pleased. "It was
a pleasure," she said, and she waved
as the kitten scrambled up and out
of the sandy burrow.

Outside it was a chilly grey day. The kitten shivered, and then shook himself.

"I'll soon be back!" he said. "I'll keep close to the hedge, and I'll be there in no time at all. Won't Mother be pleased to see me! We can snuggle up and have breakfast together. **Mew!** I'm so hungry!" And he began to hurry along, purring as he went.

"Cuckoo! Cuckoo! Cuckoo! Help me! Help!

Oh, won't anyone help me?"

The kitten froze.

The voice was coming from above him, high up in the hedge.

"Please! Please help me!"

The kitten peered up between the leaves. A feather floated past his nose, and he sneezed. "**Atchooo!**"

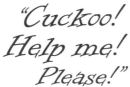

"Cuckoo!
Help me!
Please!"

The kitten shook
the feather off.
"Meeow!
I'm coming!"
he called, and
he began to
wriggle in
between the
twigs and
the branches.

They grew closely together, and
there wasn't much room for even
a little kitten.

"Ow!" he said. "Ouch! Meeow!"
but he kept struggling upwards until…

Pop!

Out he came at the top.

"Oh no!" said the voice, "you're
a CAT! Oh no – now I'll be eaten and
Father will be *furious*!"
The kitten opened his eyes
very wide.

A big blue grey bird was lying flat on his back in a neat little best. His legs were waving in the air, and he was trying to flap his wings – but he was, very definitely, stuck.

"Whatever are you doing?" asked the kitten.

"Can't you see?" said the bird crossly. "I'm stuck! I've been here for ages, and I can't move. Hurry up and eat me."

"But I don't want to eat you," said the kitten. "I came to help you."

"Are you sure?" The bird sounded surprised.

"Quite sure," the kitten said. "What can I do?"

The bird waved his legs again. "Pull me out, of course," he said. "I told my dad I needed a bigger nest, but he just wouldn't listen. He said he and Mum had always made them this size, and it was my fault for growing so big. Here, grab a leg and heave!"

The kitten balanced himself on a branch, and took hold of one of the blue grey bird's skinny scaly legs.

"I'll count to three," said the bird. "Ready? One – two – three – pull!"

The kitten pulled –
and heaved – and
hauled and…

Crash!

The bird shot out
of the nest and he
and the kitten tumbled
down to the ground
in a flurry of leaves
and feathers.

"**Ouch!**" said
the kitten, and he
rubbed his head.
The bird began to
strut about, shaking
his feathers.

"Coo!" he said.
"Did you see me fly?"

"Er … yes," said the kitten.

"I'm a star at flying!" said the bird. *"Cuckoo! Cuckoo!* Best flyer ever, that's me! Cuckoo bird, and pleased to meet you. *COOOOOOOO—* I'd better go and find Mum and Dad!"

"Yes," said the kitten, and he rubbed his head again.

The cuckoo peered at the kitten with his beady black eyes.

"Hey – what's up with you? And what are you doing round here anyway?"

"I'm going to find my mother," said the kitten. He sighed. "I'm just not sure which way to go."

The cuckoo hopped up onto a twig.

"Why didn't you say? I'll find it for you! I'll fly up in the air. *Cuckoo!* I can see everything from up there!"

The kitten sat down. "Oooh yes! Yes, you could!"

"So what am I looking for?" asked the cuckoo.

"A hedge," said the kitten. "A hedge like this one."

The cuckoo clicked his beak. "Tut! Tut! There are hedges everywhere!" he said. "Why don't I look for your mother?"

The kitten nodded. "That would be good."

The cuckoo hopped up to a higher twig. "So what does she look like?"

"Like me," said the kitten. "Stripy with white paws. And she's got a white tip to her tail. Just like me."

"Easy!" said the cuckoo. "You wait here. I'll be off and have a fly around. I'll be back in no time."

"Thank you," said the kitten.

Cuckoo bird hopped higher up the hedge. "See you soon," he said, and he stretched his wings.

"Here I go!
Cuckoo!"

And the kitten
saw him stagger,
and then flap
steadily up and up
into the sky.

The kitten watched until the cuckoo
was a small speck, and then he curled
up in the dead leaves.

"I hope he finds Mother soon," he thought. "I do miss her so much. And I'm SO hungry. But maybe she's found the very special place for us to live … our very special place where we'll be loved and hugged … and live for ever and ever …"

And the kitten began to dream a happy dream.

Seven

The kitten woke up with a jump. He hadn't really meant to go to sleep. He'd just meant to have a little rest while the cuckoo found his mother, but he was very tired, and very hungry.

But where was the cuckoo? Surely he should have come back by now?

The kitten stared up into the sky, but all he could see were white fluffy clouds.

"Cuckoo! Cuckoo! Cuckoo!"

The kitten jumped again. There was a loud flapping of wings, and the cuckoo landed beside him with a thump.

"Coo! Did you see that landing?" The cuckoo was looking very pleased with himself.

"Yes," said the kitten. "It was very clever. It was very clever indeed … excuse me, but did you see my mother?"

"What?" The cuckoo tweaked a tail feather into place. "Oh, yes. She's not far away. She was sitting on a wall in front of a house, a big place. Thought you said you lived in a hedge?"

The kitten was breathless with excitement. "You saw her? Are you sure it was my mother? Did you tell her I was coming? Did you say I was here?"

"One
thing at
a time!"
The cuckoo took
a step backwards.
"Certainly looked like you.
White paws."
"Oh – yes! Yes! That's my mother!"
The kitten was trembling all over.
"Did you talk to her?"
"Didn't like to go bothering her,"
said the cuckoo. "She was being stroked

by one of those humans – but we can be there in no time at all! Come on! It'll only take ten minutes to get there. Follow me!" And the cuckoo began to get ready for take off.

"Wait!" The kitten scrambled after the cuckoo. "How will I follow you? I can't fly!"

"Listen, little four paws – you're talking to the best flier in the world," the cuckoo said cheerfully. "I can fly fast, and I can fly slow. I can fly forwards, and I can fly backwards Just keep your little peepers open and shout if you get left behind."

"Oh! Oh!" The kitten could hardly speak. "Oh, thank you – thank you so much! Can we go now? Can we go this minute?"

"Certainly can," said the cuckoo, and with a swoop and a swerve and a dip and a dive he was up in the air above the kitten's head. *"Cuckoo!* Here we go!"

It was a good deal longer than ten minutes before the kitten struggled out of the long grass.

He was worn out, and so hungry that his tummy was hurting. The thistles in the field hurt his paws, and prickly burrs clung to his soft fur, and the grass was so long that he had to push his way through. The cuckoo flew above him shouting, "Not far to go now!" and, "Keep going, little four paws!" but it was a long, hard journey.

When he finally struggled out and saw a wooden fence in front of him he gave a faint **"Mew!"** and collapsed in a heap.

"Cuckoo!" called the cuckoo. "Little four paws! Don't give up now!"

The kitten looked up. "I want my mother!" he said, and two huge tears rolled down his nose.

"Don't cry, little four paws – don't cry!" said the cuckoo, and he flew over the fence and round to the steps by the big house front door. Two children were making a fuss of a big stripy cat with white paws, and the cat was purring loudly.

"Cuckoo!" shouted the cuckoo at the top of his voice.

"Cuckoo! Cuckoo! Cuckoo!"

The kitten tried to heave himself back up onto his feet. His legs wobbled badly, but he took a few staggering steps.

"Mew!" he said feebly. **"Mew!"**

"Poor little thing!" said a voice, and the kitten was scooped up and cuddled.

He struggled for a moment, and then shut his eyes. It was warm and comfortable … but where was his mother?

"Put him in a basket," said another voice. "Fat Freda'll look after him."

The kitten felt himself carried along and up some steps, but his eyes were much too tired to open and see where he was going.

He was gently put down somewhere very soft…

… and then he heard the most wonderful sound in the whole, wide world.

He heard purring, and the purring was coming closer. And closer. And closer.

"Mother!" whispered the kitten.

And as a long, pink tongue began to lick him clean he gave a little happy sigh and went to sleep.

Eight

The kitten with no name was warm
and cosy and comfortable. He
wasn't in the fields any more. He
wasn't under a gorse bush. He wasn't
in a rabbit burrow. He wasn't even
under the hedge where he had lived
with his mother since he was born. He
was tucked up in a fluffy rug, and he
could hear a steady purring from the
other side of the basket.

"There's Mother," he thought
sleepily, and he opened his eyes.

The big cat with white paws opened
her eyes at exactly the same time.

"Good morning, my dear," she said.
"Did you sleep well?"

The kitten's eyes opened wider
and wider. For a moment he could say
nothing at all.

It looked like his mother. Very, very
like his mother.

The white paws were the same. Even the purr was the same kind of friendly growl.

But it wasn't his mother.

The kitten sat up, his heart thumping. "Meeow!" he said.

"Who are you? Where am I? Where's my mother?"

Fat Freda didn't answer. She gently lifted the kitten out of the basket and dropped him down beside a saucer of bread and milk. "Breakfast," she said.

The kitten paused for a moment, but the smell of the bread and the milk was too much for him. He ate and ate, and when he had eaten so much that he couldn't manage a single drop more he stopped and licked his whiskers.

"Mew," he said.  "Where am I?"

Fat Freda was cleaning her paws, but she stopped to pat the top of his head. "P'rrrrr. You'll feel better now," she said. "Haven't you come to live here? I thought you were the new kitten."

The kitten sighed. "I'm lost," he said sadly.

"Lost?" Fat Freda said. "Why, you poor little thing."

"Yes," said the kitten, and he told

Fat Freda how he had walked all the way from his house under the hedge, and how he was looking for his mother.

"I've been miles and miles and miles and miles," the kitten said. "The mouse and the frog and the rabbit and the cuckoo all tried to help me, but I don't think I'll ever find my mother again. And I'll never find my house under the hedge either."

Fat Freda stood up and stretched. "What did you say your mother looked like?"

"Just like me," said the kitten. He looked at Fat Freda. "And like you. My mother's tail has a white tip too."

"Fancy that," said Fat Freda, and she settled down again in a patch of sunshine. "One of my kittens had a white tip to her tail."

"Oh, she's not a kitten," said the kitten. "She's my mother!"

Fat Freda yawned. "All my kittens are grown up now," she said. "You'll see Big Tom soon. He's one of my kittens. And Kitty Purr is another. She lives at the very top of the house with Granny Annie. Well, she used to, but she went away. Nobody's seen her – MEEOW!"

"What is it?" asked the kitten. Fat Freda was looking wide awake for the first time that morning.

"Never you mind," said Fat Freda. "You just curl up and have a rest. When the family come home from shopping they'll all come rushing in here, but you mustn't mind them. They don't do any harm."

"Oh," said the kitten. He looked at Fat Freda. "Are you going away?"

"Not very far," Fat Freda said. "I'll be back soon."

The kitten watched Fat Freda stroll out of the kitchen. It seemed very big and empty now he was on his own; even the basket didn't feel as warm and cosy as it had done. He hopped out, and looked around.

"Woof! Woof woof woof!
Woof! Woof woof woof!"
"Yap! Yap yap yap yap!"

The kitten froze. The barking was outside, but it was getting nearer.

His fur stood up on end, and he gave a tiny hiss.

He hurled himself across the carpet as the back door opened and a huge monster dog and a smaller toothy dog came dashing in. A rush of children and grown-ups and parcels and packages and bags came after them.

The kitten leapt behind the squashy old sofa and flattened himself against the wall. Then he saw a little pink basket hanging on the radiator. Without stopping to think, he dived inside and lay there, quaking with fright.

The noises in the kitchen gradually settled down. The two dogs flumped down in front of the fire, and the grown-ups pottered about clattering things and putting them on the table. The children chatted to each other, and laughed, and the kitten began to listen to what was going on.

"Is Granny Annie coming down for tea?" asked a voice.

"No, she's too sad," someone answered. "She walked down to the shops to see if anyone had seen Kitty Purr, but nobody had."

"Kitty Purr's been missing for ages now," said another voice. "I don't think she'll ever come back."

"I wish we could find Granny Annie a new cat," said a boy's voice.

"It's a shame there weren't any kittens in the pet shop."

The kitten pricked up his ears and – very carefully – he peeped out of the basket. He was almost sure that he had seen the boy before.

"Daisy B's got a pretty kitty," said a squeaky little voice. "Granny Annie can play with my kitty."

"Daisy B, you have not got a kitten," said the boy "Stop pretending you have."

"Daisy B *has* got a kitty," said the little squeak.

The kitten's ears twitched.

He remembered now. A long time ago the boy and the little girl had found him playing by his hedge, and the little girl had wanted to take him home. Was this her house? The house where she lived? The tall boy had hugged him, and his mother had said that hugs were good. But what else had she said? The kitten's ears drooped. His mother had told him he must never ever go away with anyone, and here he was in the little girl's house. He sank down again in the little basket. What was going to happen to him? Whatever was he going to do?

He crouched down in the little pink basket.

"Kitty! There's my kitty!"

There was a loud clatter in the kitchen. Daisy B had got down from the table, and was running to the door.

"Daisy B!" said a grown-up. "You haven't finished your sandwich!"

"Heard my kitty," said Daisy B, and the kitten heard the back door open.

 105

"Oh." Daisy B was nearly crying.
"Isn't my kitty. Is *BIG* cats!"

There was a sudden silence.

There was a **meow**, and then another.
Fat Freda was calling to the kitten …

… and another cat was calling too.

The kitten froze. Then he leapt out
of the little pink basket—

"Mother!"

And this time it really
was his mother.

She sprang towards him with a huge "MerrrUP!" of joy, and licked him and purred over him and rolled him over and over with her paw until he was so dizzy that he didn't notice that all the people in the kitchen were laughing and cheering and clapping their hands.

Ross was shouting,

"It's Kitty Purr! It's Kitty Purr!
She's come back – somebody tell
Granny Annie!"

Daisy B was shouting,

"It's Daisy B's pretty kitty –
he's come home!"

The kitchen door opened, and
Granny Annie came hurrying in with a
huge smile on her face.

"Kitty Purr!" she called. "Kitty Purr!
Oh, wherever have you been?"

The kitten's mother ran to Granny
Annie, and wound round and
round her legs, purring loudly.

The kitten watched
her go, and for a second
he felt lonely. But then
Daisy B picked him up.
She hugged him and
she hugged him,
and it wasn't
too tight. It
was exactly
the right sort
of hug.

And that's how the kitten found his home.

Did he find his name?

Oh yes…

Daisy B sometimes called him her very own Pretty Kitty … or Tiger … or Fluffy Paws…

But the kitten didn't mind.
He'd found his very special home
where he could live happily ever after.